Jam Jar Genie

For Quinten and Elliot, my awesome nephews

S. H.

For Cat

R. W.

EGMONT
We bring stories to life

Book Band: Purple

Lexile® measure: 570L

First published in Great Britain 2017
by Egmont UK Ltd
The Yellow Building, 1 Nicholas Road, London W11 4AN
Text copyright © Sam Hay 2017
Illustrations copyright © Richard Watson 2017
The author and illustrator have asserted their moral rights.
ISBN 978 1 4052 8310 6
www.egmont.co.uk
A CIP catalogue record for this title is available from the British Library.
Printed in Singapore.
63209/1

MIX
Paper
FSC FSC® C018306

Jam Jar Genie

Sam Hay

Illustrated by Richard Watson

Reading Ladder

Ethan didn't like Saturday mornings.
Saturday mornings meant one thing:

SHOPPING!

'Go find a trolley,' Mum said. 'Make
sure it hasn't got wonky wheels.'

'They *all* have wonky wheels,' Ethan
said as he went to fetch one.

Ethan just couldn't get excited about shopping. He liked action, adventure . . .

Zooming down hills on his bike.

Skidding around the skate park on a super-fast skateboard.

Jumping over ramps on his roller blades.

Pushing a wonky trolley around the
store just didn't cut it.

'Oh look,' Mum said. 'There's Pam.'

Ethan groaned. Pam was Mum's best friend. Whenever they got together time stood still. *Yak! Yak! Yak!*

'I'll make a start,' he said. He grabbed Mum's list and the shopping trolley.

Mum's list said to get raspberry jam.

Raspberry jam?

Bleurgh!

Ethan HATED raspberry jam. He hated the way the itty bitty seeds got stuck in your teeth. Ethan liked black cherry jam best. He looked over his shoulder.

No sign of Mum. Great! He'd get black cherry instead.

But the black cherry shelf was empty.

Well, almost.

Ethan peered into the darkest, dustiest corner and right at the back stood a single jar of black cherry jam.

The jar looked odd. It had a weird orange label with swirly patterns that seemed to move when Ethan stared at them.

Ethan picked the jar up and wiped the cobwebs off on his T-shirt. As he did this, a strange thing happened. The jar turned hot.

RED HOT.

'Yow!' Ethan's fingers burned. He dropped the jar.

CRASH!

It shattered into a zillion pieces.

'Uh-oh.' Ethan looked around.
Had anyone noticed?

But the aisle was empty.

A cloud of thick, purple smoke rose up. Ethan coughed. His eyes stung. Then he spotted something in the fog that made his heart stop all together . . .

A face!

As the fog cleared, Ethan saw that the face belonged to a strange little boy with skin the colour of carrots.

'Hi,' the boy said. 'My name's Genie!'

'Uh?' Ethan blinked a few times.

'Because you rubbed my jar and set me free,' Genie said, 'I grant you three wishes.'

Three wishes? Ethan didn't stop to ask what a genie was doing inside a jam jar. He was too busy thinking of the cool stuff he could wish for.

Like a rocket-powered pedal bike.

Or a super-sonic skateboard.

Or even his own helicopter.

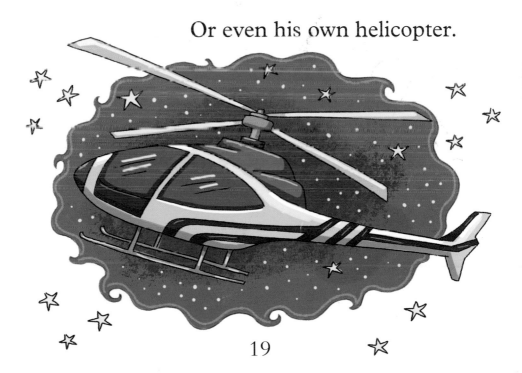

Genie clambered up into the toddler seat on Ethan's trolley. 'Supermarkets are SO dull,' he said.

Ethan nodded. 'I come here every Saturday. I wish it was more exciting.'

Genie's eyes glittered.

Ethan realised what he'd done. 'Nooo!'

He slapped his hand over his mouth. 'I didn't mean that.'

'Too late.' Genie grinned. 'You said you **WISHED** this supermarket was more exciting . . . well, I grant you your wish.'

The grocery trolley shot forward
and left scorch marks all along the aisle.

'Whoa!' Ethan tucked his feet up on the
bar and held on tight.

The wind whistled through his hair and
the shelves passed by in a blur.

Shoppers stopped and stared.

'FASTER!' Genie shouted as they
screeched around the corner of
the aisle on two wheels.

As they entered the next aisle, fizzy pop bottles began erupting like volcanoes.

'Wow!' Ethan said as a sweet,
tasty rainbow appeared above them.

Lemonade raindrops dropped on his face.
'Mmm . . .' he said, licking his lips.

The trolley splashed on through the pop puddles.

Ethan couldn't believe his eyes. The shop was alive with weird stuff.

Crazy trolleys raced up and down – dragging their customers with them.

Tins of food rolled around the aisles.
Some had even grown arms and legs
and were chasing terrified shoppers.

And animals! There were animals
EVERYWHERE!

Hens
laying
eggs.

Giant
rabbits
munching
at the
salad
counter.

And monkeys swinging from the lights.

'Hey!' Ethan ducked as one monkey threw a peach at him.

Then he heard a loud
'ROOOAAAARRR!'

'Ahhh! A LION!' Ethan gasped.

'Don't panic,' a man said, stepping forward with a fire extinguisher. 'I'm the supermarket manager. I'll sort this out!'

'The lion's going to eat him!' Ethan yelled at Genie. 'Make it stop! I wish you'd stop that lion.'

'OK,' said Genie.

One of the giant freezers began to shudder. There was a loud cracking noise, and . . .

The freezer burst open, scattering frozen
peas and fish fingers across the floor.
And out climbed . . .

38

'...*a woolly mammoth?*'
Ethan said.

39

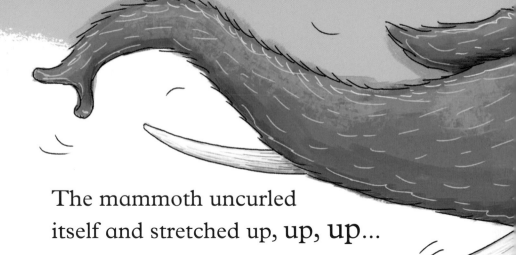

The mammoth uncurled itself and stretched up, up, up...

BUMP!

It hit its head on the ceiling and bellowed, crossly.

The supermarket manager fainted.

The lion hid behind the doughnut counter.

The mammoth thundered across the shop, crashed through the exit door and out to the car park, taking half the wall with it.

'What if it squishes Mum's car?' Ethan shouted. 'She'll go mad!'

'Wish for something bigger to catch the mammoth,' Genie suggested. 'How about a T-rex?'

'NO WAY!' Ethan said. But he had to do something.

'I wish I'd chosen *raspberry jam*,' he said firmly.

Genie's face turned red.

'I WISH I'D STUCK TO MUM'S LIST,' shouted Ethan, 'AND CHOSEN RASPBERRY JAM!'

'But I'd still be inside my jam jar,' Genie wailed.

'Yes,' said Ethan. 'And none of this would have happened.'

A cloud of purple smoke appeared.
Ethan shut his eyes. He heard a click,
like a clock being reset. Then . . .

'ETHAN!'
Mum said.
'Stop day-
dreaming and
put that jam in
the trolley.'

Ethan opened his eyes.
The shelves weren't squidged.
There were no monkeys swinging
overhead.

Had he dreamed it all?

Ethan looked up at the black cherry
jam jar on the shelf. He saw a sad little
face peeping out. Genie! So it HAD all
happened!

Genie was blowing on the inside of the glass jar, steaming it up. Then he wrote something on it.

S-O-R-R-Y

Ethan smiled.

Hanging out with Genie had been kind of fun . . . *the super-fast trolley ride, the fizzy pop volcanoes, the lemonade rain . . .* Maybe if Ethan let him out again he wouldn't get quite so carried away next time.

'Can we take two kinds of jam,' Ethan asked. 'Raspberry *and* black cherry?'

Mum smiled. 'Well, seeing as you've been so helpful...'

Ethan picked up the jar and winked at Genie. Saturday shopping trips would never be boring again!